To Babi Bang

First U.S. edition 2013

Library of Congress Catalog Card Number 2012942657
ISBN 978-0-7636-6572-2

12 13 14 15 16 17 SCP 10 9 8 7 6 5 4 3 2 1

Printed in Humen, Dongguan, China

This book was typeset in Future T Light.
The illustrations were done in mixed media.

Candlewick Press
99 Dover Street
Somerville, Massachusetts 02144

visit us at www.candlewick.com

Puffin Peter

Petr Horáček

CANDLEWICK PRESS

This is **Peter**.

This is **Paul**.

Peter and Paul
were the best of friends.

Paul made Peter laugh by being
funny and noisy. They spent their
days happily fishing around
their rocky island.

One day,
while they were

out diving . . .

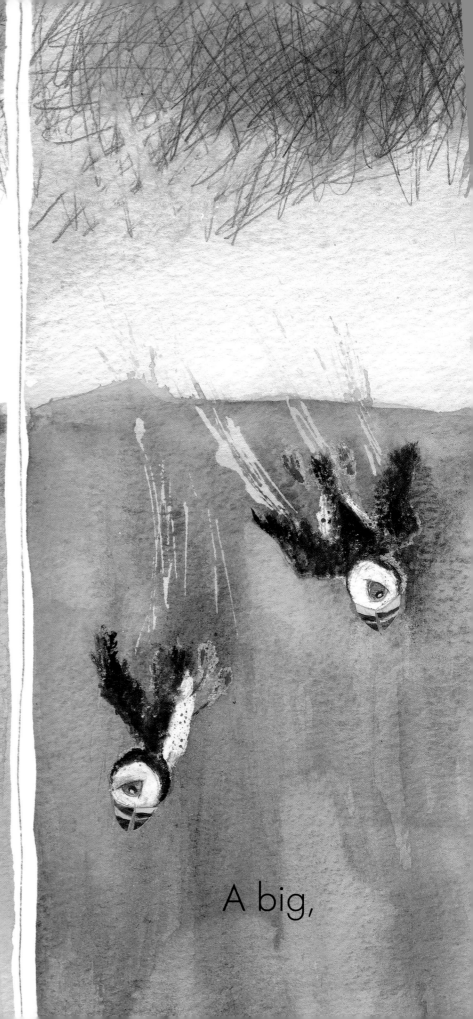

a storm

blew up.

A big,

big storm.

Peter was lost.

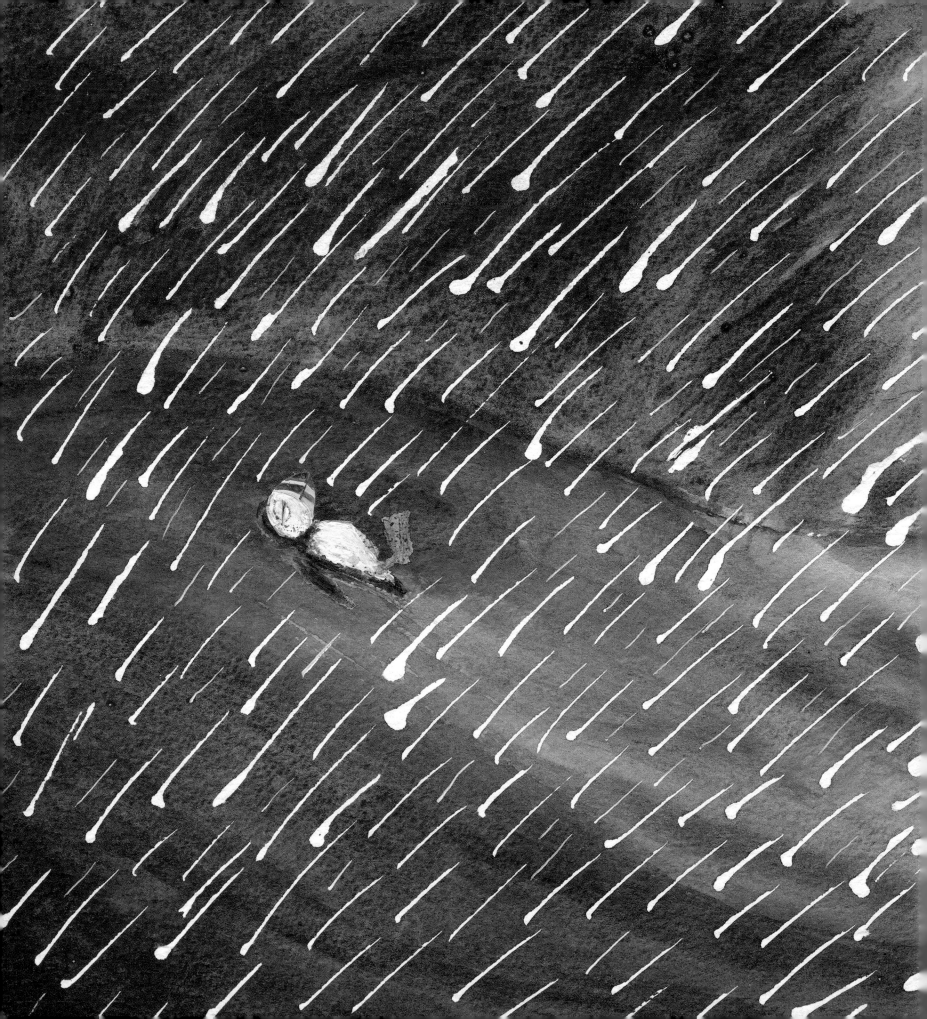

He was

blown far out

to sea.

At last the storm was over.

"Where am I?" said Peter.

He opened his eyes.

"And where is Paul?"

"Hello,"
said a large blue whale.
"Are you lost?"

"Yes," said Peter.

"And I've lost my best friend, Paul."

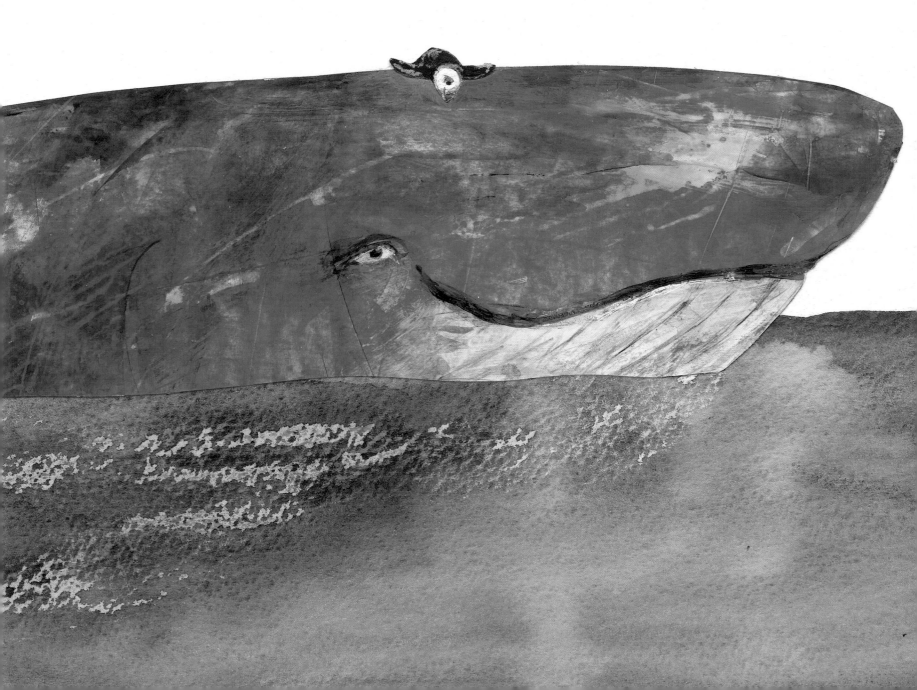

"What's he like?" asked the whale.

"Oh! Paul is funny and noisy.

Can you help me find him?"

"Funny and noisy. I know just
where to look," said the whale,
and they set off together.

They arrived at a small island.

"Which one is Paul?" asked the whale.

The birds were funny and noisy,

but they were *nothing* like Paul.

"Paul is not a parrot,"
said Peter. "Paul's feathers
are black and white!"

"Funny, noisy, and black and white?" said the whale. "I know just where to look." And off they went. The place they came to was very cold.

The birds were funny, noisy, and black and white, but they were *nothing* like Paul.

"Paul is not a penguin," said Peter.

"Paul's beak is very colorful."

"Funny, noisy, black and white, with a colorful beak," said the whale. "I know exactly where to look." And they set off again. The next bird they saw was funny, noisy, black and white, with a colorful beak, but he wasn't Paul.

"Paul is not a toucan," said Peter.

"Oh, we are never going to find him!"

Peter was sad.

The whale didn't know where
else to look, so they drifted
across the ocean.

After a few days, some tiny islands

appeared on the horizon.

Peter didn't even look up

as they drifted closer.

"Look!" said the whale. "What's that?"

It was

black and white,

with a

colorful beak.

It was
funny and noisy. . . .

It
was
Paul!

Peter was overjoyed.

"So this is Paul," cried the whale.

"Why didn't you tell me?"

"Tell you what?" said Peter.

The whale smiled.

"That he's a puffin, just like you!"